Bantam Books in the Choose Your Own Adventure® series
Ask your bookseller for the books you have missed

SKATEBOARD CHAMPION

BY EDWARD PACKARD

ILLUSTRATED BY RON WING

BANTAM BOOKS
NEW YORK • TORONTO • LONDON • SYDNEY • AUCKLAND

RL 4, age 10 and up

SKATEBOARD CHAMPION
A Bantam Book / April 1991

CHOOSE YOUR OWN ADVENTURE® is a registered trademark of
Bantam Books, a division of Bantam Doubleday Dell Publishing
Group, Inc. Registered in U.S. Patent and Trademark Office
and elsewhere.

Original conception of Edward Packard

Cover art by Catherine Huerta
Interior illustrations by Ron Wing

ISBN 0-553-28898-9

Published simultaneously in the United States and Canada

Bantam Books are published by Bantam Books, a division of Bantam Double-
day Dell Publishing Group, Inc. Its trademark, consisting of the words
"Bantam Books" and the portrayal of a rooster, is Registered in U.S. Patent
and Trademark Office and in other countries. Marca Registrada. Bantam
Books, 666 Fifth Avenue, New York, New York 10103.

PRINTED IN THE UNITED STATES OF AMERICA

OPM   0 9 8 7 6 5 4 3 2 1

SKATEBOARD CHAMPION

WARNING!!!

Do not read this book straight through from beginning to end. These pages contain many different adventures that you may have on your way to becoming a skateboard champion.

From time to time as you read along, you will be asked to make a choice. After you make your decision, follow the instructions to find out what happens to you next.

Think carefully before you act. Skateboarding can be fun, but it can also be dangerous. You'll learn some skills you've never even dreamed of. But be prepared for unexpected adventures—in this book, you'll have them! To help you in your adventures, a glossary of skateboarding terms and phrases is included on the following pages.

Good luck!

GLOSSARY

Aerial, air walk—taking off; losing ground contact.

Backside—turning so your backside is upslope as you come around.

Boneless—planting your foot and using it to bound upward.

Deck—the main part of the skateboard.

Drop—skating off an elevated surface.

Fakie—skating up a surface and sliding down backward.

Frontside—turning so you're facing upslope as you come around.

Grind—skating on a narrow surface on the *trucks* of your board.

Halfpipe—a 180-degree concave skating surface.

Handplant—going *aerial* and arresting and redirecting your descent with your outstretched hand.

Invert—being inverted in the air, supported only by a *handplant*.

McTwist—a spectacular 540-degree *aerial* spin.

Ollie—jumping over or onto an obstruction without your feet leaving the board.

Slaloming—a winding or zigzagging movement downhill.

Slide—sliding or skidding on your wheels, or on the wooden underside of your board.

Truck—the mechanism connecting the wheels to the *deck*.

Vert—skating on a vertical surface.

Wall rides—riding up a wall or a concave surface.

Wheelie—riding on the back wheels.

Your family has just moved to Park City, California. Although you like the house a lot, you find that it's a little small. It's also going to take some getting used to the traffic and the noise of the neighborhood, which is in an old part of town. Your dad has told you there's a lot of crime in Park City and warned you to be careful about where you go and the people you spend time with.

A couple of weeks ago you started classes in the Jefferson School. So far you're not sure that you like it very much. There are a lot of tough kids there, and some of them have been giving you a hard time. As much as you'd like to fit in, you find that your classmates are somewhat cliquish. You sense that if you don't join up with at least one group, you will find yourself being "out of it" altogether. You've been sort of feeling your way around, trying to decide which kids you'd like to become friends with.

There's one group around school that seems really interesting—the skateboarders. A lot of them skate to school and keep their boards in their gym lockers. Although they tend to have wild haircuts and wear weird clothes, some of them are real interesting to talk to. Their leader, Steve Gordon, can do some tricks that you can hardly believe. You have a board yourself, but you really haven't skated that much. If only you could get half as good as Steve Gordon is!

Turn to page 2.

2

One thing you've noticed is that most kids around school don't seem to think much of the skateboarders. They treat them as if they were diseased or something.

You wish things weren't so split up. Unfortunately they are, and you're just going to have to live with it. As you think about how to fit in, you realize that what you really want to do is join up with the skateboarders. On the other hand, there's another club at the school called the Winners' Club. Only a few kids are selected to join it each year, and the club president has told you he thinks you're really cool. They want you to join, but it's clear that if you do, you can't hang out with the skateboarders. You won't be able to do both; you're going to have to choose one.

If you decide to join up with the skateboarders, turn to page 12.

If you decide to join up with the Winners' Club, turn to page 89.

Saturday, right after lunch, Brad and Billy pick you up in a rusted old Honda. One of your skateboarding friends, Sid Hargraves, is in the back, along with an older girl named Felicia, whom you've seen around school.

Billy tells you that it's a long drive to the pool, but it will be worth it. However, once Brad heads out of town and drives for what seems like forever along some country road you've never even heard of, you begin to wonder if he knows where he's going. After all, he drives fast, doesn't talk much, and what he does say isn't very intelligent.

You're beginning to wish you hadn't come along when Brad turns up a long paved driveway that winds through the woods and up a steep hill. As the car reaches the top, you see a big wooden house set in the middle of a beautiful lawn.

"Gee, who lives here?" you ask.

"You don't need to worry about that," Brad says. "There's no one around. They're off in Europe or someplace like that."

"Well, are you sure it's okay to—"

"Don't be a wimp," Brad interrupts. "Just wait until you see what's out back."

One by one everyone piles out of the car and heads around the side of the house. There's a huge wooden deck in back, and inset into it is a very large kidney-shaped pool. Brad and Billy peel back the plastic cover. The pool is empty, and the inside is clean and deep and has the most beautiful curved surface you've ever seen.

Turn to page 57.

4

There are about six guys and several girls racing around the incline of the fountain. You join the action, skating as hard as you can. It feels good, but most of the time you're trying to keep from wiping out. You need to practice a lot more before you can just relax, giving in to the freedom that skateboarding brings.

A couple of the kids start whistling. They're looking over at the blur coming down the walkway—it's Steve Gordon. He's made the most out of a little incline and is racing toward the fountain. He glides up the ramp and takes to the air in a frontside invert. Planting a hand on the rim, he holds his board with the other hand and just kind of hangs up there. Then he arches down, back on his board, and glides around the ramp. He makes it look so easy.

Everyone's watching as he goes back up the ramp and does a high aerial, then a backside turn. Slamming onto the deck, he glides to the opposite side and takes to the air again, this time doing a little air walk. Coming down, he does a fantastic McTwist before he eases down the ramp, picks up his board, and strolls over to chat with one of the girls.

Turn to page 13.

6

Steve's house is only a couple of blocks from yours. It's an old two-story frame house with steps leading up to the front porch. A cement driveway leads to a garage that is badly in need of a paint job. Steve takes you around to the backyard, about half of which is taken up by an empty swimming pool.

"Wow, you can skate in that?" you ask.

"Yeah," he says. "I made a deal with my folks: as long as I pay for any damage to the pool, I can use it for skating when it's empty."

"With a deal like that you could go broke."

Steve is grinning. "I doubt it—I already made five thousand bucks doing commercials for Dazzler Skateboards."

"Wow, but I'm not surprised," you say. "I saw those routines you were doing."

Steve grins at you. "Would you like to learn how to do some of them?"

"That would be fantastic."

Turn to page 84.

You know you could skate circles around this goon, but you don't like the idea of wrecking someone's pool, even if you can get away with it. You don't bother answering Brad. Instead you walk over to take a closer look at the damage. Right away you can see that the whole thing will have to be resurfaced and will probably cost several thousand dollars at the very least.

Well, you think, if it's got to be resurfaced anyway, it won't hurt if you scratch it up a little more. Still, you have your doubts. Maybe you ought to just sit this one out.

If you decide to skate in the pool,
turn to page 74.

If you decide against it, turn to page 73.

8

You've never been so happy as you are now, skating back home from the First Federal Bank Building. All kinds of nice thoughts are going through your head. In another year you and your friends will have professional competition ramps and halfpipes. For the first time in your life you feel like you have a chance of becoming a world-class pro—a skateboard champion.

The End

You feel terrible about what happened to Patti, and very angry at the hit-and-run driver. If only you'd had a skateboard—you could have caught up with the car and gotten the license plate number.

As you think about the events of the day, you decide to quit the Winners' Club after all and take up skateboarding to school from now on.

Pretty soon afterward, you make friends with Steve Gordon. Steve is definitely the best skater in school, and you feel flattered when he tells you one day that he thinks you've got natural talent. He says if you worked at it, you could become a great skater. He volunteers to coach you but says, "There's no point in doing it unless you're willing to go all out. You'd have to practice at least a couple of hours a day."

"I'll let you know tomorrow," you say.

That night you lie awake, trying to decide what to do. It's one thing to skate to school and back and have a little fun at it on the side; it's another to practice two hours a day. That sounds like a lot of work. Still, Steve's offer is very tempting.

If you decide to take lessons to improve your skateboarding, turn to page 84.

If you decide to just stick with what you've been doing, turn to page 92.

You hop off your board, flip it up into your hand, and walk inside. Immediately there's a gun in your ribs, then a hard shove and a snarling voice.

"Flat on the floor, *now!*"

The other men who walked in ahead of you have put on ski masks. One of them is talking to the teller. The other two are guarding the customers, forcing them to lie on the floor.

You lie down as you are told, keeping your skateboard close beside you. You keep your eye on the man you recognized. The teller is passing him stacks of money, and he's shoveling it into his suitcase. Suddenly he turns and starts toward the door. As he passes the customers lying on the floor, his eyes come to rest on you.

One of the other robbers yells at him, "Hurry! We've got to get out of here!" But the man whips his pistol around. Instinctively you swing your board in front of your body. It only shields part of you, but it catches two bullets; another one grazes your shoulder.

"Are you crazy?" the other robber says furiously. "We have the money. Let's get out of here!"

Together they run, and in a moment they're out the door.

Turn to page 62.

12

You decide to follow your heart and go with the skateboarders. The next day after school gets out, you see one of your new friends, Jack Lombardi, getting his skateboard out of his locker. "Any good places for skating around here?" you ask.

"Sure," he says. "On the way to my house there's a new shopping center going up. They've got a lot of cement inclines and ramps—you just take your pick. You do any skating?"

"I have a board," you say. "But I really need to work on my technique."

"Have you seen Steve Gordon?"

"Yeah, he's something."

"I've seen him do an eight-foot vert off the base of the fountain in Bradshaw Park."

"I'd like to see that," you say.

"Well, we're going to work out over there tomorrow after school. Bring your board—you can join us. I'll see you there." With that Jack looks both ways down the hall. The next second he's on his skateboard, weaving around a bunch of girls. Startled, they make faces and call him names.

As he approaches the outside door, Jack hops off his board. It flies up in front of him; he grabs it with one hand, opens the door with the other, and in half a second is outside. That's just as well, because Mr. Flynn, the gym teacher, has spotted him. "Hey Lombardi!" Mr. Flynn calls, trotting after him; but Jack is already out of sight.

Turn to page 53.

You exchange glances with Jack Lombardi. "I didn't know anyone could skate like that," you say.

"Steve told me he's going pro next year. We may not see too much of him then—he may be out on the circuit, making sixty or seventy thousand a year."

You stand there shaking your head.

"Awesome, huh?" You turn around to see who's talking: it's Erica Lind. Word is she's the best girl skater in town.

Turn to page 48.

14

You yank off your shoes and helmet, take a deep breath, and jump into the water after Steve. In an instant you're under, kicking, trying to slow your fall. Your feet hit a rock on the river bottom, and you push off hard, shooting up to the surface.

Steve's head is sticking out of the water. He's paddling feebly with one arm, barely keeping afloat. You grab his skateboard, which is drifting steadily downstream, and swim toward him, kicking furiously. You shove the skateboard under his hand. "Hold on to this," you say. "I'll help you to shore."

He grins, but his grin quickly turns into a look of pain. There's no question he's hurt—it's just a matter of how badly.

Remembering what you learned in lifesaving class, you cup your hand under Steve's chin and paddle him toward shore. The water is so cold it might as well be filled with icebergs. You paddle harder, but you feel yourself tiring. The human body can't last long in cold water. But you know, if you stop to rest, you'll never make it to the river-bank.

Turn to page 63.

Despite Steve's warning about the danger of skateboarding in this town, you decide to put everything you have into improving your technique. Your hope is to get as good as Steve was, perhaps even better.

Some people in Steve's place might be bitter over being stuck on the sidelines while you're out having a great time, but not Steve. He isn't like that at all. He gives you every tip he knows in order to help you become a champion. With his coaching, and your daily practicing, you begin to learn all of the flashiest tricks in the book. You become a master of fakies, grinds, slides, and ollies, and even more exotic tricks like the fabulous McTwist.

One day when you finish practicing, Steve comes up and shakes your hand. "Who would have believed it?" he says. "You're better than I was!"

That night you go home feeling a warm glow. It's as if you'd graduated from skateboard university. You are good, you know that. And you feel like showing off your skills for everyone to see. But part of you feels more humble. Perhaps you should just keep to yourself and work quietly at becoming a pro.

If you decide to let people see you in action, turn to page 31.

If you decide to work quietly toward becoming a pro, turn to page 34.

You try to flag down a passing car for help. The first one zips by without stopping, but the second one, a red VW Jetta, screeches to a halt.

"Someone's fallen off the bridge!" you yell.

"I'll call the police," the man behind the wheel says. What a break—the guy's got a cellular phone.

It turns out he doesn't need it. Seconds later a police car pulls up behind the Jetta, lights flashing. An officer gets out. "What seems to be the trouble?"

"My friend fell off the bridge—actually he was forced over!"

As you say this, you run to the wall and look down into the swirling waters twenty feet below. You see a skateboard floating upside down in the water, but no sign of Steve. The officer and the Jetta driver join you.

"When did this happen?" the policeman asks.

"There he is!" the driver shouts, pointing to a spot downstream.

You see Steve flailing with one hand, trying to remain above water. "I'm going in after him," you say.

The policeman already has his shoes and jacket off. "Direct traffic until more police arrive," he tells you. Then he leaps off the bridge, hitting the water feet first.

Turn to page 69.

The largest one of them comes up real close to you and just stares blankly. "When you get that thing fixed, maybe you'll come back and teach us some of them tricks," he says.

"Maybe we can make boards ourselves," another says. "There's lots of scrap around here."

"You can help us," another says.

"Sure . . . I'll be glad to," you say.

By the time you get home, it's way after dark. You explain to your folks what happened, and how you had to walk all the way home from River Flats.

Your dad looks at you kind of strangely, as if he doesn't know whether to be angry over what you did, or glad that you're home.

"You're not to go over to that area again," your mom says firmly. "It's much too dangerous."

"You've got a point, Mom," you say, "but—it's a funny thing—the most dangerous guys there are now my friends."

The End

After thinking about what happened to Steve, you decide that you're just headed for trouble if you continue skateboarding. The next day you hang up your board on the wall opposite your bed, get a regular haircut, and start dressing like the other kids.

Just when things seem to be settling down, your mom and dad tell you that they can't afford to send you to college unless you can help out by saving up some money on your own as well. "The reason we bring this up now," your dad says, "is that Mr. Beck, the owner of Beck's Pharmacy, mentioned to me this morning that he needs a messenger for a couple of hours a day. It would make a good after-school job. You'd deliver prescriptions to people in the neighborhood, mostly older people who can't pick them up themselves."

Your mom looks at you intently. "It would mean a little less TV and video games and fooling around with the gang," she says, "but if you start saving money now, it will amount to quite a lot by the time you're ready for college. It would help out a great deal."

It doesn't take you long to think this over. "I'll do it," you say.

Turn to page 50.

Paul grunts again, then looks around nervously as his buddies all watch him step onto the board and start down the ramp.

He doesn't get going very fast, but even so he can't stop. At the bottom he twists violently, landing in a heap.

As Paul gets up, his buddies laugh. You keep an absolutely straight face—you're no dummy.

Paul starts up the ramp, board in hand. Quickly the other guys quiet down. There's anger in Paul's eyes, and he's limping a little. Obviously he's a bit shaken, though he's trying not to show it.

"This ain't much good—keep it, dude," he says, shoving the skateboard into your arms.

You're grateful to get your board back. "I took a lot of bad spills when I was learning," you say.

Paul only grunts and mumbles something you can't understand. You figure now's the time to get on your way.

"Well, so long," you say, scooting off before they have time to react.

"Hey!" you hear Paul call out after you. "The next time you come back here, maybe you'll teach us a few of those tricks?"

You call over your shoulder, "Sure," but you know it's the last you'll see of them. From now on you're going to stay away from River Flats.

The End

The next morning the police have two suspects in custody. You go down to headquarters and identify them. They were the men in the white Camaro, all right. You also identify the guy who shot at you as being the one involved in the jewelry store robbery several months before.

To save his own skin, one of the robbers confesses, informing on the crooked policemen who were protecting the racketeers. You're not surprised to learn that they were the same two cops who gave you a hard time for skateboarding instead of chasing down the jewelry store robbers.

You're thrilled to get a $5000 reward for your help in breaking up the crime ring. But even better, you're proud to know that from now on Park City will become a much nicer place to live.

The End

You don't give it another second of thought—you whip around the corner and scoot through an alley. There's a ramp at the end of it, leading down to the highway. Seconds later you're careening down the ramp. It curves upward to the top of a cement retaining wall.

You've gotten up plenty of speed now. You travel up the ramp, take to the air, and plant a hand on the top of the wall, then down onto the barrier on the other side. You gather a little more speed and do a drop to the sidewalk running along Woolsey Avenue.

The bridge is just ahead of you. In a few seconds you're on it, weaving through the traffic. You're not sure whether you've come out ahead of the white Camaro or behind it until you hear the sound of tires screeching behind you. An engine is accelerating, and it's coming directly at you. Just like Steve Gordon, you're on the bridge with nowhere to go!

Over the bridge is a twenty-foot drop into the water—at this time of year it's hardly above freezing. You can either jump, or—there's one other chance—ollieing onto the sports car just ahead of you. Whatever your decision, you have to make it now!

If you go off the bridge, turn to page 111.

If you ollie up onto the roof of the sports car, turn to page 28.

The nurse grins at Steve. "You just keep quiet if you want to get out of this place," she says.

"How's my temperature today?" he asks.

"A hundred and ten," the nurse says with a straight face as she inspects the thermometer.

"Gee, if I'm that hot I should definitely get more ice cream."

"Go on with ya!" the nurse chimes back, gathering up her equipment and marching out of the room.

"We carry on a running battle," Steve says. "I think she likes it as much as I do." He smiles, probably for the first time since he was hurt, you think.

"I'm a little confused," you say. "Do you think I should quit skating or not?"

Turn to page 37.

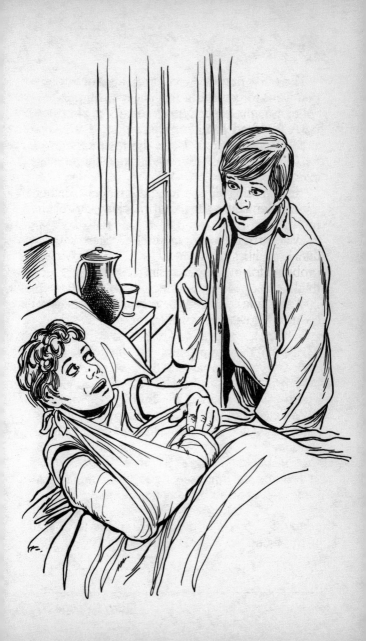

When you visit Steve in the hospital the next day, you meet his sister, Claire, in the waiting room. She thanks you for rescuing Steve but gives you some bad news.

"Steve is going to be in the hospital quite a while," she says. "The doctors say he'll be okay, except . . ."

"Except what?" you ask hesitantly.

"Except his skateboarding days are over. In time he'll be able to walk and even run pretty well, but they say there's no chance he'll be able to skate the way he used to."

You shake your head. "That stinks. I'd like to get my hands on the guy in the Chevy that ran him over the edge. Steve would never have lost his balance if it weren't for that car."

"The police mentioned that to us," Claire says. "They think it was probably just an accident that the car swerved when it did."

"I'm not so sure of that," you say evenly. "I'd like to try and find out the truth."

While Steve's in the hospital, you visit him almost every day. You're really impressed with his attitude; he doesn't feel sorry for himself at all. "You've got to take life as it comes," he says. "I've had some great times skating and I'm sure I'll have some great times now doing other things."

"Well, you inspired me," you say. "I'd be really happy if I could get even close to the level you were skating at."

Turn to page 70.

You and the other Gamma Rays head over to the park to do some skating. Some of the guys do tricks on the ramp around the fountain, but no one's really very good at it. Mostly you just try to see how many people you can scare by skating right at them and then, at the last moment, veering off to the side.

Everywhere you go people stare at you. There are a lot of old people in the park, and some of them shake their fists and insult you. Matt always deals with this by skating past whoever it is and giving them a big smile. "It's a free country," he says.

After a while, skating in the park is no longer very pleasant. A number of cops are now hanging around. One day they move in on the group and tell all of you to beat it.

"Hey, let's try the ramps down at the square," Matt says.

He leads the way, and you and the others follow, although you trail a little behind. By the time you get there, the others are doing grinds on the court-house steps. You stand back and watch when suddenly a bunch of cops surround them, and a paddy wagon pulls up to cart them away!

Turn to page 97.

It's not often a skateboarder has a chance to catch a ride on a Porsche, but this one has been slowed down by traffic. Scooting after it, you gain speed very quickly, then ollie up over the spoiler and onto the top of the car.

Suddenly you're falling through the sunroof! You land right next to the astonished driver, a young woman with long blonde hair. She shrieks and almost swerves into another car. By the time she gets control of her car and back in her lane, you're sitting very properly, holding your skateboard in your lap.

She gives you an icy look. "What are you doing here? You're lucky you're still alive. You know you'll have to pay for scratching up my car."

You glance back—the robbers are accelerating toward you. "Neither of us is going to be alive if you don't get us out of here," you say.

The blonde glances in her rearview mirror. She sees the same thing you do—a man leaning out of the Camaro with a gun, waiting to get close enough to shoot.

Suddenly you're thrown back against your seat as the Porsche accelerates. Then it swerves around a Dodge pickup and zooms along the other side of the road, heading straight toward oncoming traffic! A scream builds up in your throat, but the Porsche swerves again, darting into a tiny space between two cars on the right.

Turn to page 95.

You're about halfway down the driveway when you round a curve and see a car coming at you, head on—it's another cop car! It brakes, and so do you! You're going about thirty miles an hour and there's hardly enough room for both you and the car. As you whip by, you almost take off the side mirror. You make it past, and you're still standing! You can't believe it.

You can hear the car accelerating. The drive is so narrow, it'll have to go up to the house before it can turn around again and come after you. You should be able to make it to the end of the drive-way by then. Maybe you can take off into the woods across the road. They'd probably never find you. On the other hand, perhaps you should stop and talk to the cops. After all, you are innocent.

If you try to escape, turn to page 79.

If you stick around to face the cops, turn to page 80.

The next day after school you take off down the street, ollie over a curb, and scoot over to the ramps in front of the library. When you get there, you speed up the wheelchair ramp and take to the air, do a boneless handplant, then do a backside wall ride into the garden. The people sitting on the park benches stare in amazement as you go by. Another bench is empty, and you ollie over it. How'd you like that, folks? you wonder, as you whip around the corner.

And then . . . *SMASH!* The little old lady you've just crashed into goes sprawling onto the ground! As she hits the curb, you hear something crack.

"Gee, ma'am, I'm really sorry!" you say, rushing to help her. You pick up her eyeglasses and lay them gently on her purse.

A crowd quickly gathers around to help. Most of them are yelling at you, calling you all sorts of names and phrases as the poor woman writhes and moans on the ground.

A policeman comes up. "Stay right where you are!" he barks.

"I'm awfully sorry, ma'am," you say again, as the policeman puts in a call on his radio.

Turn to page 72.

Felicia skates off, leaving you standing there alone watching. It is then that you notice that your fears have been realized: the skaters are badly scratching the whole inner surface of the pool!

You watch Brad do a handplant on the edge of the pool and land on his feet, holding his board with one hand. He looks a little shaky and almost loses his balance. He's a good skater, but obviously out of shape.

He sees you watching him. "What's the matter with you?" he calls. "Butterflies in your stomach or something?"

Turn to page 7.

For the next year you keep working quietly at your technique, hoping to turn pro. More and more kids have gotten into skateboarding, and some of them are quite impressive.

One day you and two of your friends decide to build a competition ramp in your backyard. You work at it really hard on Saturdays, sharing the costs and labor. By the time summer vacation comes around it's ready.

Working out on your new ramp, you find your verts are soon higher than ever. You're able to develop a smoothness and a style that you never had before. By the end of summer vacation, you feel like you're on your way to greatness!

One day you're skating around town with two of your buddies, Shane Rorabock and Jack Lombardi. The three of you are doing slides down the railing in front of the public library when Jack spots a cop headed toward you. You take off in a hurry, managing to get away without being caught.

As you reach the top of the hill at the Wentworth intersection, Jack says, "Hey, let's race down to the bottom. Last one to reach Stan's Soda Shop buys the others a Coke."

Go on to the next page.

You look down Wentworth. It's pretty steep. There are a lot of curbs to cross, and there's a lot of traffic. You know if you don't stop in time for the traffic lights, you can count on a truck rolling over you.

Shane looks at you skeptically. He doesn't want to be the chicken in the group, but you know he'd probably be relieved if you said, "Forget it." It seems like the choice is up to you.

If you decide to race, turn to page 99.

If you decide not to, turn to page 40.

"Hey, you, get down off that board, and stay off," one of the cops says.

"But I haven't been doing anything wrong," you protest.

"You're creating a nuisance and endangering life and property," he says.

"That's not true. This is a public park. I always practice here, and I'm always cautious."

"If we catch you here again, we're bringing you in."

You're so mad, you just pick up your board and walk away. You find a bench on the other side of the park and sit down while you try to decide what to do. There's only one other place in town you know of to practice—an abandoned ramp leading to the expressway along the river. It's in a part of town called River Flats. The trouble is that it's a really tough neighborhood, the sort of place where you could run into trouble. Maybe you should just give up skating altogether, you think.

Dejected, you get up, hop on your board, and start toward home. You're still not sure what to do, but as far as you can see, you've got three options.

*If you decide to keep skating in the park,
turn to page 101.*

*If you decide to try skating in River Flats,
turn to page 105.*

*If you decide to quit skating altogether,
turn to page 112.*

Steve lies there with his eyes closed. After a while he says, "The truth is, I don't know. Skating in this town is dangerous, and I think it's going to get even more dangerous. On the other hand, when you're in the air, sailing over the top of the ramp, you just don't think about those things—you just feel great."

As you stand there looking at Steve, you think about how much you'd like to become a skateboard champion. The more you think, however, the more you wonder if it might be a lot smarter, and safer, to quit.

If you decide to quit skateboarding,
turn to page 19.

If you stick with it and try to become a champ,
turn to page 16.

One day on your way home from work, you're walking up a steep hill at the top of Wentworth Avenue, holding your board in your hand until you reach the other side of the incline. You've almost reached the top when you hear the sound of several gunshots being fired! A moment later two men run out of a jewelry store across the street from you. They're holding guns in one hand and satchels in the other. A maroon Comanche van screeches alongside them; the men jump in, and the van takes off down the hill you just climbed up. Several cars slow down, or manage to pull over to the side, but no one stops. It all happened so fast!

You peer down the hill after the van. It's already a block away, and the license plate is so dirty you can't see the numbers.

Turn to page 52.

"We don't need to race, Jack," you say. "We already know I'd win."

Shane and Jack make caveman sounds when you say this, but you don't hear them—you're already on your way down the hill, but at your own pace. You don't need to get yourself killed just to prove something!

On your way home, you realize you've got a big decision to make. The school year is about to start up again, and the question on your mind is whether you should keep devoting as much time to skateboarding as you've been doing. Unless you're going to go all out and become a skateboard pro, it's not really worth it, you realize. That means entering tournaments, going to skate camps, meeting promoters, getting coaching— and lots more practice. It would be hard to keep up with your schoolwork. However, if you *could* get to be a world-class skateboarder, you'd have a lot of fun, get to travel a lot, and make a lot of money—all at the same time!

If you decide to try to turn pro, turn to page 56.

If you decide against it, turn to page 58.

Van Neff smiles at you. "You see, I'm not that worried about damage done to my pool. What I'm worried about is that so many kids seem to be getting into trouble in this town. I want to know if you have any suggestions about what can be done to help prevent this."

"Well, I don't really know, Mr. Van Neff," you say, "but I do have one idea. I think it would be great if kids could have a special place they could go to skateboard. That would keep a lot of us out of trouble."

Van Neff tilts back in his chair and gazes out the window for a moment. Then he fastens his keen blue eyes on you. "You know, my young friend, I think that's an excellent idea. I'm going to recommend it to the City Council and tell them I'm willing to help raise the money to build it."

"That's terrific, sir. That's really great."

Turn to page 8.

As you round the curve at top speed, you brake hard when you see what's up ahead: two guys, both at least half a foot taller than you, waiting for you at the bottom! One of them is on each side of the ramp, and they're holding a rope between them, ready to snare you if you try to get past.

You back up to the curve and look toward the top of the ramp. Two more guys are waiting there for you, armed with heavy sticks.

You're trapped! There's only one possible escape —to do a grind down the wall alongside the ramp, then, just before you reach the guys with the rope, hop on your board and do a drop to the pavement ten feet below. If you and your skateboard are still in one piece after you land, you could probably get away from these guys before they catch you.

Of course, you could break your neck. But if you're not willing to take the chance, you'll just have to face these guys and hope for the best.

If you try to escape, turn to page 61.

*If you try to deal with these guys,
turn to page 67.*

The years pass. One day your dad announces that he's been offered a great job in Aspen, Colorado—he'll be managing a big ski resort there.

"You've got a surprise coming," he tells you. "You're going to be able to skateboard right down the mountain, except your board won't have wheels. It will be called a snowboard!"

"That sounds great," you say.

Soon you find out just how great it is. In Colorado, snowboarding is a fast-growing sport. Because of the skills you've developed as a skateboarder, you learn fast. Within a year you're an expert. And in the years after that, you just keep getting better and better. As you go down the mountain people point to you and say, "There goes a real snowboard champion."

The End

Meanwhile the four big guys run down the ramp and surround you. Slowly they move in closer. You think of using your broken skateboard as a weapon to defend yourself, but you know it wouldn't do you much good in its present condition.

The big guys suddenly stop, no longer making a move. In fact, you can see by their expressions that they were impressed with your performance.

One of them then reaches over for your skateboard. "Let me see that, dude," he says, taking it out of your hands.

"How'd you learn to do that?" another one asks.

"You just need a good board and a lot of practice," you say.

"Looks like this one's got to go back in the shop."

"Yeah," you say. You can't believe you're having this conversation.

"Hey, you shouldn't be jumpin' off walls like that," the other one says. "You could hurt yourself."

You nod. "Yeah, that was kind of dumb of me."

The guys start to laugh, and soon you're laughing too, more relieved than amused.

Turn to page 18.

"We're not interested in any van, kid," the cop says. "Come over here, now!"

You trot up to the car. "But officers—that van! Didn't you get a call about a robbery? A man's been shot. That van is the getaway car!"

The cop gets out of the car slowly and walks over to you. "We don't know anything about any van," he says menacingly. "We just know that you're a public nuisance. Take some advice, kid. Don't do any more skateboarding around here or you're likely to end up just like that other kid—the skateboard champ. Know what I mean?"

You don't say anything; you just can't believe this is happening.

The cop walks back to his car and gets inside. A moment later he and his buddy drive off, turning left at the intersection, in the opposite direction of the van! That settles it—you're certain now that these cops must be protecting the criminals. You wish you could prove it, but you don't see how.

That night you have a lot of trouble sleeping. This town's not a healthy place to live in, you realize. Unless you give up skateboarding completely, it's going to get even unhealthier as far as you're concerned. As much as you want to hang up your skateboard, however, part of you wants to hang in there and see what you can do.

If you decide to give up skateboarding, turn to page 59.

If you refuse to quit, turn to page 71.

"I wish I had the talent to skate like that," you say.

"You do," Erica says. "I watched you skate—you've got terrific balance, you just don't have your technique down yet."

"You know the secret," Jacks says. "Practice."

Up comes a short kid with dark hair about a foot long—Pete Martinez. "Hey, you guys, let's drift down to Camelot's for a Coke."

Seconds later you're all on your boards, racing along the walkway toward the northeast corner of the park. You watch Pete ollie over a bench, then over a trash can. He's almost as good as Steve is.

As you reach the street, you wait for the traffic to go by before crossing. From behind, you hear a sound. An orange and black blur is coming toward you. Suddenly Steve is standing there.

"Hey, I was watching you," he says. "You could be a really good skater if you worked at it."

"Thanks," you say. "Want to join us for a Coke?"

"Next time," he says. "I got to get home and practice on my ramps."

"You have your own ramps?"

"Better than that. Want to come over and see?"

"Sure," you say, telling your friends you'll catch up with them later.

Turn to page 6.

50

The job at Beck's Pharmacy starts out pretty well. Mr. Beck pays you by the hour at a very low rate, but he makes up for it by giving you a small bonus for each prescription you deliver.

This seems fair enough at first. But after a couple of weeks you haven't really made that much money—it just takes you too long to get around and make each delivery.

But then an idea hits you. You can make a lot more deliveries by using your skateboard. By carrying the prescriptions in your backpack, you can skate to each address. You can cut across courtyards and over low walls and in general travel around faster than you can on a bike! And you don't have to worry about leaving your vehicle—if your delivery is in an apartment building, you can take your board up in the elevator with you.

One morning, as you're getting ready to go to school, you take your board down from the wall. Your mom gives you a long look. "Have you quit your job?" she asks.

"No, this is to *help* me on my job," you say, going on to explain your plan.

"Well, be careful!" she says, scowling.

Turn to page 109.

You realize it's best to remain quiet. Obviously there's nothing you can say that will help. You climb into the back of the squad car, then head for the station house.

You sulk for most of the ride, but after a while you say, "You want to keep us out of trouble, but there's not much for kids like me to do in this town. There ought to be a place we can go—a place where we can skate, for instance."

Neither of the cops replies, but when the car stops at a red light, the driver turns around and says, "You know, kid, you got a point."

"Don't worry, kid, you'll probably get off with a warning," the other cop says. "But maybe you ought to think about taking up another sport from now on."

"You know," the driver says to his partner, "what these kids need is a specially built skateboard rink. The city ought to build them one. Then we wouldn't have these kinds of problems."

"Let's recommend it to the chief, and maybe he'll put some pressure on the mayor," says the other one.

You feel a little better now after having this conversation. It's been a bad day, but maybe some good will come out of it yet.

The End

Seconds later the jewelry store owner runs out into the street, yelling and waving with one arm for help. His other arm hangs limp at his side. He's bleeding from his shoulder, you notice. A car screeches to a halt and someone jumps out to help the wounded man. There's not a cop anywhere in sight.

You glance down the hill again. You can still see the van—it's about three blocks away now, but it's stuck at a red light. If only you could get there before the light changes.

Without stopping to think, you plant a foot on your skateboard and scoot faster and faster until you've gotten up *real* speed. Then you go for it, down the hill, slaloming through the traffic. A couple of astonished drivers honk at you—they must think you're crazy, and maybe you are, but you're determined to catch that van before it gets away!

Turn to page 66.

The next morning you decide to skate to school. Your board is in your hand as you walk out the door.

"Going skateboarding after school?" your mom asks.

"Thought I might—the school yard's pretty good for that."

"As long as you don't skate on the street," she calls after you. "And be careful."

As you turn your corner, safely out of sight, you drop down your board, step on it, and keep scooting until you've gotten your speed up. Soon you're racing down the sidewalk, keeping your eyes open. As you reach the curb, you look both ways, ollie onto the street, and skate across. At the opposite curb you lose your balance and have to jump off your board. You feel kind of awkward, but at least you didn't fall. Your balance is good, you just need practice.

After school, you join Jack Lombardi and a bunch of other kids and head down to Bradshaw Park.

When you reach the big plaza in the center, you see all the skateboarders standing around in the concrete dish surrounding the fountain. If it were summer, they'd be sloshing around in six inches of water, but the fountain's off now for the fall, and the concrete around the inside is perfect for skateboarding, curving up at just the right angle.

Turn to page 4.

You run toward Patti, who is sprawled out on the ground, not moving. A crowd has gathered around her.

"Hit-and-run!" someone shouts, running for help.

Glancing down the road, you see the car braking sharply. It's stuck in traffic at a red light about a block away. You run after it, hoping you'll get close enough to read the license plate number before it gets away. But the light changes, and the cars start to move.

You're almost close enough to see. If only you could run faster! The car finds an opening and leaps ahead. You lose sight of it as it whips around a corner.

You hurry back to Patti, just as a police car screeches to a halt. Two cops jump out. One of them rushes to her, and the other calls out to the crowd standing around, "Are there any witnesses here?"

You step forward and describe the accident and the car that hit the girl.

The cop shakes his head and reaches into his squad car. He grabs the radiophone and broadcasts a description.

A couple of minutes later an ambulance pulls up. The paramedics jump out, and you watch them carry Patti to the ambulance on a stretcher. You give the cop your name and address, then continue on your way home.

Turn to page 9.

Once you've decided to try and turn pro, you become very disciplined about practicing and keeping in shape. You know that in all sports the great champions make their skills look easy. To bring that off they can't be easy on themselves; they have to work hard, striving for perfection every day.

There are times when you feel like quitting, when you're sailing ten feet in the air, doing a perfect McTwist, you know that your hard work has been worth it. When spring comes, you decide it's time for you to try out for the national championships.

All of this seriousness doesn't mean that you don't still like to have fun. When one of your skateboard pals, Billy Karsten, tells you about an empty swimming pool that any skateboarder would drool over, you're eager to know the details.

"You'll see what I mean when we get there," Billy says mysteriously. "Let's go Saturday afternoon. My cousin, Brad Mullin, has a car. We can catch a ride there with him."

You've never met Brad Mullin, though Billy's spoken about him. From what you remember, he's several years older than you and kind of wild. You guess it doesn't really matter much what he's like, just as long as he takes you over to try out that pool.

Turn to page 3.

"What are we waiting for?" Billy shouts, already on his board and over the edge. Brad joins him in a flash. Seconds later they're doing verts off the other side.

You turn to Felicia and Sid, who are still standing by the side of the pool. "Do we really have permission to do this?"

"I don't know. I guess it's okay with the owners," Sid says. He shrugs and scoots off on his board, warming up with a turn around the perimeter of the pool.

You exchange glances with Felicia. "Brad learned about this place because his cousin's in the pool cleaning business," she says. "They service this pool. Last week they emptied it and covered it because the owners—the Van Neffs—were going away on vacation." She drapes her polished fingernails thoughtfully over the front wheels of her board and gives them a spin. "Guess I'll do a few runs in the shallow end. Come on!"

Turn to page 33.

58

As much as you love skateboarding, you don't want to make it your whole life. The next day you take down your skateboard ramp, giving your mother the space she's been wanting for a flower garden.

You still skate to school in good weather, and occasionally you take a turn around the fountain in the park, but you stop hanging out with skateboarders and start going in for other sports. Soon your schoolwork improves, and your teacher tells you that there's a good chance you'll be able to get a scholarship for college.

Turn to page 81.

That night you hang up your skateboard for the last time. You had a lot of fun with it; it was a great sport, and you made some friends you wouldn't have met otherwise. You even made a good deal of money on your job skating. But now it's time to move on to other things.

Turn to page 45.

You skate up the wall, and into the air with your board in one hand. Dropping the board crosswise under your feet, you come down on the top of the wall, then grind down the ledge toward the bottom of the ramp.

The guy waiting for you at the bottom is extra large—he looks like a pro football player. He watches you wide-eyed as you come toward him, shocked at what you're doing. He leans over the ramp, ready to grab you, but you don't plan to ride the wall that far.

You get your wheels rolling again and build up a little more speed. Then, just before you reach him, you take to the air, still riding your board. You compress your body to absorb the shock, preparing yourself to land on the pavement below.

The impact wrenches your gut, sending waves of pain through your body. Every muscle in your legs is stressed to the limit, but you stay on your board—you made it! You start to build up your speed again, but as the board rolls forward a couple of feet, it stops and tilts so sharply that you have to hop off.

You pick it up and examine it. The forward truck is half broken off, and it's dangling at a crazy angle, like a bird with a broken wing.

Turn to page 46.

One by one the customers get to their feet and start to leave. But the manager, who has been hiding behind the counter, shouts at them, "Everyone stay here, please! The police are on their way, and they need to talk to all of you as witnesses."

Your skateboard saved your life, no doubt about that. But right now you're feeling more angry than scared. You want to see where the robbers went; this time you're going to get their license number!

You race outside. The manager calls after you to come back, but you don't even turn around.

A dirty white Camaro is pulling away from the curb with a terrific screech. It's the getaway car! You memorize the license number, but you have a feeling the car is stolen. The robbers will probably abandon it as soon as they can.

You glance around. Where are the cops? Well, you're not going to wait around for them. Seconds later you're on your board, weaving through the clogged traffic, chasing the white Camaro.

You don't have a downslope this time—you're going to have to use your brains instead of speed. You figure the Camaro will almost surely get stuck in traffic if it keeps on down this street. More than likely it will turn onto the Woolsey Avenue bridge. You doubt the robbers will stop to switch cars until they're across the river.

Turn to page 23.

You hear someone yelling. You glance over your shoulder and spot a man on the bridge—you're glad someone's seen you. The current, however, is carrying you faster now. You try stroking, but the cold has drained the strength from your body. You're going under!

As you start to sink, your feet touch bottom. You lunge forward into shallower water, and manage to get Steve up to the bank. He looks white as a sheet, and he can't stand up—he must have hit something underwater when he fell.

"You're okay now," you say, putting your coat over him for warmth, even though it is wet.

He tries to thank you, but once again pain takes over his face.

Suddenly an amplified voice calls from up on the bridge, "STAY WHERE YOU ARE. HELP IS ON THE WAY."

You look up and see the flashing lights of a police car. Standing on the bridge is an officer holding an electronic megaphone.

Steve's eyes are closed, but he seems to be breathing all right. "Hang in there, pal," you say. "You're going to be okay."

Moments later you hear the wailing of an ambulance.

Turn to page 26.

Unfortunately there's a lot of hostility toward you, and not just from adults. Many of the kids look down upon the skateboarders. Some of the skaters even seem to resent you for your seriousness. As for the people in the park—there isn't a day that goes by when someone doesn't insult you.

You're tempted to tell these people what you think of them, but you know that wouldn't do you any good. Instead you keep to yourself, being extra careful and trying to avoid skating near old people, little kids, or people walking their dogs. As far as you're concerned, you're a perfect citizen. Nonetheless, a couple of cops come up to you one day while you're doing grinds on the edge of a ramp.

Turn to page 36.

Coming upon a red light, you realize you've got to stop! You're going really fast; you have to drag the tail of your board until it's practically smoking. There are no cars coming, thankfully, only a trailer truck lumbering along. You'll have no problem beating it.

Coming to a stop, you then scoot up to speed again and whip across its path! The driver honks at you, but you're home free. It's now clear boarding to the bottom of the hill. You're quickly closing in on the van. But then the light changes. The van cuts right, turning south on Main.

You ollie up onto the sidewalk, aiming for a ramp that slopes up to a wall near the intersection. If you can get onto that wall, you'll have a good view of the van as it comes down Main.

The van completes the turn, but it's blocked by a truck. Suddenly it cuts hard right and goes up onto the sidewalk! A man drops the newspaper he's reading and leaps for safety.

As you're getting up onto the wall, the van swerves over the next curb and back onto the street. Then you hear a siren behind you. You glance back—it's a cop car, flashing its lights.

The cops turn up onto the sidewalk now, taking the same route the van did. Then the car brakes to a stop. There are two cops in the car, you notice, and one of them is yelling at you.

"Hey kid, come down off that wall!"

"Officer!" you yell. "Get that van—the robbers are in it!"

Turn to page 47.

You decide to deal with these guys—you just have to keep your cool. You take a deep breath and start skating down the ramp. The guys at the bottom have the most surprised looks on their faces. They never thought you'd plow straight into the outstretched rope.

Instead you surprise them by ollieing up into an aerial twist, then coming down with your board at a right angle to the slope. Then you lean uphill, digging the upper edge of your board into the concrete and braking to a stop inches before you reach the rope.

"Hi-ya, guys," you say, trying to sound calm as you hop off the board.

"That's some show," one of them says.

The largest one of the group comes up real close to you. "That's a real nice board you got there. I think I'll take it."

"It's the best there is," you say, realizing it's smart not to argue. "I think you'll like it."

You hand over your board, trying to appease him. He grunts, then looks a little puzzled when he takes it.

By now the other two guys who were at the top of the ramp have joined the three of you. One of them taps the big guy on the shoulder. "Come on, Paul, show us what you can do."

Turn to page 21.

The policeman bobs up in the water and looks around.

"That way!" you say, pointing toward Steve. The policeman heads toward him, but he's not a very good swimmer. By the time he reaches Steve he's in trouble himself.

"Wait here," you tell the Jetta driver; then you leap off the bridge, your skateboard in hand.

You hit the water. It's freezing, but you can't think about that now. You swim toward Steve's skateboard, grab it, and then make your way over to where he and the policeman are. "Hang on to these!" you say, pushing the boards toward them.

Steve looks deathly pale, but he manages to drape his arm over his board. The policeman takes hold of yours, and together the three of you work your way over to the riverbank.

"Good work," the officer says. "He would never have made it without you."

Turn to page 26.

Steve props his bed up with the electric control he's holding in his hand. "Look pal, not only could you get close to my level, I think you could surpass it. You're a natural. Hey, I can't skate any more, but I can still coach. I'll tell you every secret I know—except . . ."

"Except what, Steve?"

"Except I don't think this is a good town to skate in. The mob doesn't like skaters. You know that car that forced me over the edge—it wasn't an accident."

"I didn't think so, either," you say. "I saw the whole thing."

"I'm sure that someone from the mob was trying to do me in."

"The mob? But why?"

"Because I've seen too much. Last week I stumbled upon a jewelry store holdup. I could have gotten the license plate number of the getaway car if I'd been on the ball. But the point is they probably think I did get it, and that's why they're after me."

"I wouldn't think the mob would even notice a bunch of kids on skateboards."

At that moment a nurse comes in to take Steve's blood pressure and temperature. The moment the thermometer comes out of his mouth, Steve grins at her. "Hey, nurse, can you do something about the desserts around here—that ice cream last night was gone in two spoonfuls."

Turn to page 24.

You decide you're not going to let yourself be intimidated and give in. You'll keep skateboarding, come what may. Who knows—maybe you'll find enough evidence to turn those crooked cops in after all.

You continue working for Beck's Pharmacy, and making good money, though you don't race around at quite the same speed you used to. For one thing you're keeping an eye out for those crooked cops, or anyone else who looks suspicious. If someone's out to get you, you're not going to make it easy for them.

In the weeks ahead, things go smoothly. The newspapers say the crime rate is showing signs of dropping off. You begin to relax.

One day Mr. Beck asks you to deposit some checks in the bank.

"Sure thing," you say, and in a flash you're off.

You're approaching the bank on your skateboard when you see three men hurrying in ahead of you. One of them is carrying a small suitcase. He looks familiar except for a bushy mustache that seems too big for his pale, thin face. You're certain you've seen him before. Thinking how he would look without the mustache, you realize he's one of the men who shot the jeweler and escaped in the Comanche van!

As they reach the entrance, he glances around and gives you a funny look. He says something to one of the other men, then turns and enters the bank.

Turn to page 11.

Later on you find out that the lady broke her hip and fractured two ribs. It's a terrible thing to hear—you didn't think you'd hit her that hard. But it shouldn't have surprised you—old people are a lot more fragile than the rest of us.

And that's exactly what the judge tells you when he sentences you for disorderly conduct, misuse of public property, disturbing the peace, and reckless endangerment! Your sentence is five hundred hours of community service. You're going to spend all your time after school and on weekends helping elderly people in nursing homes. You'll have plenty of time for it now, you think. You've hung up your skateboard for good.

The End

You decide that you're not going to skate in that pool if you don't want to, no matter what anyone says. You stroll off to the side and lie back in one of the lounge chairs, admiring the big trees surrounding the back lawn. You wish you could go home now, but it's too far away to skate, and hitching doesn't seem like a good idea. You might as well just wait until your friends are finished.

It's no fun watching the others skate, however—none of them is really very good. To keep from being bored, you start walking around the side of the house, looking for something to do. You've just about reached the driveway when a cop car pulls up. You duck behind a bush and watch as two officers get out. They look around, taking their bearings. They must hear the noise because they start to trot around the side of the house, passing about ten feet in front of you. You'd like to go back and warn the others, but the cops would spot you for sure. The moment they round the back of the house, you race for the driveway. Seconds later you've got one foot on your board and you're getting up speed, heading down the drive. You reach the steep part, then go for it—you want to get as far away from those cops as you can!

Turn to page 30.

Once you've decided to go ahead and skate, you really let loose, trying out some of your favorite tricks. You take to the air and perform a McTwist right onto the diving board! Then you drop off the board and race along the length of the pool. The others climb out of the pool and watch. You can see them out of the corner of your eye. They didn't have any idea you were so good.

Suddenly a whistle sounds. You skate up to the shallow end and look over the edge. Oh no—there are two cops standing there.

"Out of the pool—now!" one of them shouts.

You're so nervous about what's going to happen to you that you have to get off your board and climb up the pool ladder.

"I didn't go in, Officer," Brad says, lying to one of the cops.

"You're a liar," you shout. Normally you wouldn't rat on someone, but after Brad came up with the idea, was the first one in, and jeered at you for hanging back, who is he to be playing innocent? It really makes you mad.

"Worry about yourself," the cop snarls at you. "You're the one we saw with the skateboard. You've done enough damage to require the entire pool to be resurfaced!"

He comes over and slips a pair of handcuffs on you! "Kid, you should know these houses have electronic surveillance," he says. "That might be a good thing for you to keep in mind in the future."

Turn to page 104.

Deciding to join the Gamma Rays, the next day you head down to the mall with Matt and a couple of his friends and spend more money than you intended to on weird clothes and accessories. Then you go over to Matt's house, where he gives you a haircut that you think is a real disaster, but Matt's really pleased with. Then he puts orange dye on what's left of your scalp. It's a good thing your family is really laid-back about things like this.

"Congratulations, you're a Gamma Ray," Matt says proudly. "We don't go in for any initiation stuff. Just shake hands—now you're one of us and we're one of you."

The next day you arrive at school along with the other Gamma Rays. The truth is, you'd be embarrassed to go in by yourself—you look so weird.

Most of the other kids keep clear of you. Being a Gamma Ray turns out to be a great way to lose friends.

After school, Mr. Karn, the principal, calls all of you in and warns that the Board of Education is going to ban this kind of thing. Soon you'll have to come to school dressed neatly, and with regular haircuts.

"That would be unconstitutional!" Matt Cunningham says.

"We'll just see about that!" Mr. Karn shouts, unable to contain his anger.

You feel a little shaken after this meeting, but Matt says, "Don't worry about Karn—he's all talk and no action."

Turn to page 27.

Jack and Shane skate up alongside you. "Are you all right?" they ask.

Just fine, you try and tell yourself, but the pain in your arm is killing you.

Before you pass out, you're dimly aware of the crowd around you. You hear sirens. Cops are all over the place. Out of a bruised, swollen eye you see the ambulance that is coming for you.

All your friends come to visit you in the hospital. "You're going to be okay," they all say. "You'll be skating again in no time."

Even though it hurts to move your neck, you just shake your head when they say that. With much effort you manage to work up a little grin and say, "Anyone here want to buy a used skateboard?"

The End

You decide there's no way you're going to risk facing the cops. You keep moving, tearing down the drive, weaving around fallen sticks. You can hear the cops accelerating up to the top of the driveway—you've got to get across the road before they come down again!

You crouch, lowering your air resistance, trying to pick up every bit of speed you can. Within seconds you're nearing the end of the driveway. You can't see if any cars are coming down the road, however—trees are blocking your view.

You drag your foot, trying to brake before you reach the road. Then you hear a sound—a truck is coming. You drag your foot harder, but it throws your board off course, and the wheels hit a snag. The truck whizzes by as your body flies into a hundred-year-old beech tree. You feel a stabbing pain; then you're out.

Turn to page 94.

Deciding to face the cops, you brake, hop off, flip your board up into your hand, and start walking up the driveway. You're about halfway to the top when the cop car comes barreling back down. The cops brake hard when they see you, but you jump off to the side in case they don't stop in time. They wave you over.

"Get in the back," one says.

You do as you're told, and the moment you close the door behind you, the driver backs up the hill at high speed and screeches to a stop in front of the house. He parks next to the other cop car that's already there, and both cops leap out.

"Stay there," one of them says. Then they start jogging around the side of the house. You test the back doors. You're not surprised: they're locked.

After a while the cops return, marching your friends in front of them. They shove Billy and Felicia in next to you, and Brad and Sid ride in the back of the other car.

On the way back to town, Billy explains what the cops said. "We're all being charged with malicious trespass and willful destruction of property. They said we'll have to pay for the damage we did to the pool. One of the cops said it could be over $5000."

Turn to page 93.

It turns out your teacher's right. When you finish high school, you get a scholarship to the University of Colorado! When you arrive at the campus the following fall, you find the big sport there is skiing. You've never skied before, but your skateboard training makes you a fast learner. By the time you graduate, you're skiing on the best team in the country and having the time of your life. Looking back, you realize you made the right decision.

The End

Things are really glum around school after that, until one day some of the skateboarders come to school with most of their hair clipped off. What's left is dyed orange, and they're dressed in weird clothes that look like costumes in some kind of pirate movie. Their leader, Matt Cunningham, is a real cool guy. He's smart, and he's a really good skater. You can't believe it when he asks if you would like to join their gang. "We're calling ourselves the Gamma Rays," he says. "We're going to do what we like when we like it—that's our motto."

"Thanks, but I don't know," you say. "I don't want to get into any trouble."

Matt puts his arm around your shoulder and whispers in your ear, "Gamma Rays don't get into trouble—they make trouble."

You're tempted to join the Gamma Rays. They seem to know where the action is and how to have fun. Still, maybe you should just stick to yourself for a while and work at your skateboarding technique.

If you decide to join the Gamma Rays, turn to page 76.

If you decide to work on your skateboarding instead, turn to page 98.

Taking Steve up on his offer, you listen as he starts out by giving you some important advice. "First thing you'll need to do is get yourself a pair of gloves and kneepads. No matter how good you are, you'll eventually fall. Also, any time you're doing something tricky, wear a helmet."

"I didn't think it was cool to wear all that stuff," you say.

Steve lays a hand on your shoulder. "Look, if you hurt yourself, you won't be able to skate at all, much less walk. And I'll tell you something else: you'll be more confident, and skate better, if you wear a helmet and pads."

That afternoon, you learn how to weave down the street and "pump," pushing sideways while the board is at an angle to your path of travel.

Soon you're almost keeping up with Steve as he skates around town. But when he goes off a three-foot-high concrete wall and drops onto the sidewalk, you're left behind.

"Hey, wait up!" you call. "I can't do that."

Steve comes back. "That's nothing," he says. "Just wheelie the board—let the front wheels go up as you go off the edge. Keep your weight directly over the board as you come down, and compress your body to absorb the shock."

You try it.

"Perfect drop," he calls back at you, already racing down the road.

Turn to page 108.

The ramp is banked sharply and bounded by a three-foot-high wall. The ledge at the top is almost a foot wide. You skate your heart out for about an hour, doing verts off the wall, coming down on the ledge, and then dropping onto the ramp. There are all kinds of slopes and curves, as if the place were built for skaters.

When it's time to head home, you get up speed so you'll be able to glide for a long way after you come down off the ramp.

Turn to page 42.

Twenty minutes later Van Neff's secretary shows you into his enormous office. The first thing you notice is the fantastic view from the wall of windows on both sides of the room. You can see half of Park City from here and a good deal of the countryside as well.

Van Neff, a slim, elderly man, motions for you to sit in the red leather chair across from his long wooden desk. "Thanks for coming so promptly," he says. "Let me get right to business. The police

told me that you were the only one who refused to skate in my pool. I want you to know that I admire your good character and your judgment. Because of that I wish to consult with you."

"Well, uh gee . . . thank you."

Go on to the next page.

Van Neff clears his throat, then pulls a lozenge out of a little box on his desk and pops it into his mouth. "First of all, you'll be glad to know that I dropped the charges against your friends. Instead of their paying for the pool repairs, I propose to let them make up for what they did by working an hour a day after school for a month in the Community Center for the Homeless."

"I'm sure they'll be glad to hear that, sir."

Turn to page 41.

As much as you'd like to skateboard, you decide that you'd rather join the Winners' Club instead.

It seems like a big deal at first, but after you've been hanging out with the "winners" awhile, they don't seem to be so special. And you don't really like the way they're all stuck-up and how they think they're so great.

Sometimes you see skateboarders going by, having a great time, and you wish you could be with them. What really gets you is watching Steve Gordon, a lanky, curly-headed kid who is definitely the best skateboarder in town. When you watch him down in the park, doing tricks off the ramps around the fountain, you can't help but want to step on a board and try some of that stuff yourself.

One day while you're walking home from school, you see a girl from your class, Patti Nielsen, walking about a hundred feet ahead of you. As she reaches the curb, a car comes along and seems to swerve off course, heading directly toward her! You watch her jump back, but the right fender of the car clips her, sending her flying across the sidewalk. Instead of braking, the car accelerates and takes off down the street!

Turn to page 54.

One day you and Steve are on the bridge, skating along the pedestrian walkway. On the river side of the walk is a low concave wall. Steve is about a hundred feet ahead of you, doing some tricks on the wall, taking to the air. Anyone who didn't know him might think he was on his way into the river.

You're skating along, watching, trying to get up enough courage to join Steve, when a gray Chevy whips by. It's weaving off the roadway, headed toward your friend. "The driver must be drunk!" you yell at Steve, who is heading up the ramp.

He looks back over his shoulder. The car is screaming toward him! Steve is inverted in the air, and there's no room left for him to come down! As the car scrapes along the side of the bridge, he grabs the top of the wall with one hand. A chill of horror goes through you as he loses his balance. He's falling in the river! Still weaving, the gray Chevy accelerates out of sight.

You shake your fist at the hit-and-run driver, then scoot over to where Steve went off. Looking into the swirling waters twenty feet below, you see no sign of your friend, only his skateboard floating upside down.

You can jump in and try to save him, or you can flag down a passing car and ask for help. Either way you've got to act fast!

If you jump in after Steve, turn to page 14.

If you flag down a passing car, turn to page 17.

92

You thank Steve for his offer but tell him you're not really interested in investing all that time practicing.

In the weeks that follow, you have a streak of bad luck. First, you get chicken pox. You're out of school a whole week and get behind in your work.

When you return to school, you find that the skaters aren't as friendly to you as they used to be. Maybe it's because they heard that you didn't have any ambition or desire to stick it out. Steve Gordon, however, is still friendly, even though he's the biggest skateboarder of them all. Then one day you hear in school that he was skating over a bridge when a car spooked him and he went off. He broke his collarbone and fractured his hip and would have drowned had the current not carried him onto some rocks in the middle of the river.

Turn to page 83.

Back at police headquarters, you tell your story to the investigating detective, a ruddy-faced guy with curly black hair.

"I'm not sure I believe you," he says, "but we don't have enough evidence to prosecute. I'm going to recommend that the charges against you be dropped."

"Thanks," you say. "Does that mean I won't have to help pay for the damage?"

"That's up to the owner, Mr. Van Neff," the detective says. "Whether you're charged with a crime is one thing; whether the owner wishes to sue you for damages is another."

A couple of weeks later you get a call from Mr. Van Neff himself. He wants you to come to his office after school the next day. He gives you the address—One Franklin Plaza. You know where that is. It's the First Federal Bank building, the tallest in Park City. There are some great concrete ramps along the plaza, and you've skated there many times.

When you walk inside the glass and steel tower, the building directory tells you that Mr. Van Neff's office is on the top floor. It also tells his title—President of the First Federal Bank. No wonder he can afford such a fancy house and pool!

Turn to page 86.

Later, but how much later you can't even guess, you wake up and find yourself in the hospital. Your body hurts all over. Judging by the casts and slings covering you, you know you smashed yourself up pretty badly. You'll have to wait until the doctor shows up until you know more.

You glance around the room. You must have been out for quite a while because there's a big vase of flowers on the TV set, and a bunch of get well cards on the table alongside your bed. With the hand that's not in a cast, you reach over and grab the biggest of them—it's from the kids who went skateboarding out to the pool with you. They've all signed the card, and above their names is written the following:

We're really sorry about what happened to you. We're all going to have to pay for repairs on the pool, but we told the police that you weren't involved, so don't worry about that. We miss you, and hope you get well soon. By the way, everyone's talking about you around school. They say you're a real skateboard champion.

The End

A few seconds later the blonde sees an opening.
The car leaps ahead again, reaching seventy
within seconds. Then she slams on the brakes.
Your seat belt digs into your stomach as the car
screeches to a stop. The woman leans on the horn,
drawing the attention of a police cruiser coming
toward you. You throw off your seat belt and stand
up, poking your head and shoulders through the
sunroof. The cruiser brakes to a stop.

"Someone's trying to kill us!" the blonde
shouts.

"It's the same ones who just robbed the bank—
they're in a white car!" you yell. You turn to see
the Camaro doing a wild U-turn to avoid the police
cruiser. In a flash the cops are after it!

"That was some great driving!" you say, turning
to the trembling woman beside you.

"Thanks," she says, sweeping her hair back into
place. "You mean to say they were after you because you were a witness?"

"Yeah, I don't think they wanted me around
anymore."

The woman takes a deep breath. "Well . . . I'm
glad I was able to help you. The insurance com-
pany can pay for the scratches on the roof. I'll take
you home now."

Turn to page 22.

One of the cops comes over to you. "Come on, you're joining the party," he says.

"But I wasn't doing anything," you say. "I was just watching."

"Then why are you dressed like a weirdo and wearing orange hair?"

"I'm exercising my constitutional right of free expression," you say.

Just then another cop comes along. "Is there a problem?" he asks the first cop. But before he gets an answer, he grabs your sleeve. "Come on."

"But I'm not a Gamma Ray," you protest, looking him straight in the eye. "Really, Officer."

The cop looks at you skeptically.

"The fact is that I *was* a Gamma Ray," you say very politely, "but I recently quit."

"*Very* recently, I'll bet," the cop says, putting his hands on his hips. "But since we didn't actually see you breaking the law, we'll let you go—this time."

When the paddy wagon pulls away with the Gamma Rays, you're still standing there, wondering when your hair will grow in, and how much you can get for a used skateboard.

The End

You decide to really work at your skateboarding. You watch the techniques of the best skaters around, subscribe to a skateboard magazine, and rent several videos that show some of the top skaters in action.

One day you happen to tune in on the national championships on cable TV. When you see just how fantastic some of these guys are, it really inspires you. You decide to try to become one of these championship greats.

From then on you practice like a demon. Although you don't have a competition ramp of your own, you are able to practice in the park, doing verts off the curved ramp alongside the fountain. There you can practice the tricks that you'll need to know in order to compete in big tournaments.

Turn to page 64.

"Okay, guys," you say, "I'll see you down there." You push off, quickly getting up speed. You can hear Jack behind you, but Shane is slow getting off. He's just not as gutsy as you and Jack are.

Several cars are ahead of you—they're slowing down as they come upon some construction. You slalom past them, then ollie up onto the curb to avoid a garbage truck. You can hear Jack barreling down the sidewalk across the street from you. There's a yellow light up ahead, but you know you can beat the UPS truck crossing Wentworth in time. Dropping off the high curb, you scoot across. The truck driver honks wildly but he doesn't need to brake—you're back on the street again, and it's a good long run until the next light. The steepest part of the hill lies ahead.

Turn to page 106.

The next day you're back at the park, skating happily without a cop in sight. Pushing off, you head for the ramp around the fountain. You warm up with a few frontside fakies.

As you're coming off the ramp, you see a guy in a leather jacket with a walkie-talkie. He must be a cop, you think. You get off your board and start to run out of the park.

"Come back here," he shouts. "Police!"

Climbing onto your skateboard, you take off down the walk, slaloming around the pigeons and ollieing over a couple of park benches along the way. You reach the exit from the park over on Wentworth Avenue, just as two more cops are rounding the corner—one of them is the officer from yesterday!

"Okay," he says, cutting you off. "We're going to book you, with the added charge of refusal to obey the lawful order of a police officer."

"What are you talking about?"

He points at the plainclothes cop coming toward you, the one with the walkie-talkie.

"But—" you protest.

"Tell it to the judge!" With that, one of the cops snaps a pair of handcuffs on you.

"What is this—a police state?"

"Keep talking like that, kid, and you'll be in even deeper trouble."

Turn to page 51.

Now that you're back on your skateboard again, your life starts to get in high gear. Things are going well at school, and your job is really fun now. Also, you've not only gotten back your old form, you've become the best street skater in Park City.

You've had a couple of cops warn you to keep off sidewalks, of course, and you've taken a little heat from pedestrians who think you're a menace. But you've noticed some people simply stop to watch with amazement as you ollie over curbs, do slides down the railing in front of the library, or use your aerial skills to get over a wall. Whenever there's a little slope, you're able to take advantage of it and get up awesome speed.

Mr. Beck can hardly believe how fast you've been making all your deliveries. He checks up on you by calling some of the customers to find out if they really got their packages. You're not surprised when he tells you that every one of them is pleased. They say they've never gotten such fast, courteous service before.

Most days you've finished all your deliveries well before normal quitting time. As a result you're working less, and yet you're making more money than ever!

Go on to the next page.

There is one thing, however, that worries you amidst all your happiness—the fact that crime in Park City has increased more than ever. Several times you have passed police cars lined up, their lights flashing, people crowded around. Despite all their investigations into the increasing robberies, they haven't arrested any suspects and always seem to arrive too late to prevent the thieves from getting away.

Turn to page 39.

It turns out that the final bill for resurfacing the pool comes to $5,326.50. Paying that wipes out all the money you and your parents have been saving for your college education. You even have to sell your skateboard to help kick in for the total amount. Not that you'll miss it—after what happened, you've lost your taste for skating completely.

The End

You step on your board and scoot along the gentle upslope along Claremont Street, headed for River Flats. Along the way you ollie over curbs and hydrants, limbering your legs. Then you hook a right and glide down Smith Boulevard for almost a mile, past the fancy apartments, past the old Episcopal Church, stopping only at the light across Oakland Avenue.

Now you're in River Flats. The houses and apartments are mostly run-down, the shops look poorer, and some of the people on the street look hungry.

Ahead of you are the old railroad yards, and beyond them is the abandoned ramp leading to the expressway. You cut through a vacant street lined with tenement houses and seedy-looking bars and restaurants. You pass a hefty-looking woman carrying a large bundle of clothes on her back, some old men clustered around a lamppost which they are using for support, a young boy running across a street looking as if he were fleeing for his life, and a doorstep guarded by three ragged-looking cats. As you pass a group of teenagers, you speed up. They eye you suspiciously.

"You goin' the wrong way!" one of them yells after you. But you know where you're going.

You round the corner and skate in between the oil drums that are placed in the road to block traffic, then skate up the abandoned ramp.

Turn to page 85.

106

As you race down the hill, you crouch in order to increase speed. You're definitely in first place, but you can hear Jack coming up behind you. Glancing around to see how close he is, you miss seeing a little pothole ahead of you. It's not much more than a nick in the road, but your front wheels catch on it and send you flying over the front of your board. You try to break your fall, but you hit the ground hard and then keep skidding. Cars swerve, trying to avoid hitting you. Then you hear a crash and look up to see that two cars have collided. Horns are going off all over the place but you really don't care. You're in pain, and you're bleeding. One, possibly both, of your arms is broken. You've really done it now.

Turn to page 77.

108

Steve's a good teacher, but he's tough. He tells you you'll need to practice at least two hours each day; otherwise he doesn't want to waste his time on you.

You give it your best. After a couple of months you're doing things you'd never even heard of—a backside boneless, board slides, grinds, wall rides, and even extreme verts, where you skate straight up a ramp and take to the air, doing an air walk or a McTwist before you come down.

As time goes on, you get to like your new school a lot, even though there are certain kids who look down on you and your friends for skateboarding. They don't know what they're missing, you think.

There is one problem though: there are a few guys hanging around who seem to have nothing else to do but be mean. The other day a couple of them tried to ambush you in the park. You had the feeling they were going to take your board away, possibly even rough you up. You managed to skate right by them, reach the street, and take off on the downslope. They ran a few yards after you, then gave up.

There seems to be a lot of crime in Park City. You've heard that gangsters have been buying off some of the local politicians. That may or may not be true. However, there have been several robberies in your neighborhood lately, and none of the crooks has ever been caught.

Turn to page 90.

Skating to school that day, you're incredibly happy. Your technique is a bit rusty at first, but by the time you reach your locker, you feel as if you've never been off your board. From now on you're going to make more money and have more fun doing it. You're sure of that!

Turn to page 102.

You decide to go over the bridge. After a twenty-foot free-fall, you hit the water in between a couple of cakes of ice. Your skateboard flies out of your hand; the cold hits you like an electric shock. As you continue to plunge, you try to flatten your body to keep from hitting the bottom. You graze a rock anyway and manage to push off and shoot up to the surface, hitting your head on the ice.

Throbbing cold grips your body. You thrash your way toward the shore, but you can feel yourself cramping up. You're not sure if you can make it. Your body goes numb, and your strength drains away. You feel yourself giving up as your head slips under the water.

You're going down, but you don't want to. You reach for some inner strength. When your feet touch bottom, you manage to push yourself up again. With the last ounce of strength that's left in you, you lunge forward and collapse on the riverbank.

Several people are hurrying toward you. You're going to be all right!

Maybe life will get better from here on in. You can only hope so. At the very least it should be a lot safer. When you get home you'll be hanging your skateboard up for good.

The End

Deciding to quit skateboarding for good, you sell your board to a kid you met recently who's just getting into the sport. "Good luck. I'm going out for the soccer team," you tell him.

Soccer turns out to be a good sport for you. However, when spring comes and you take up baseball, you soon become known as the strikeout king. One day the coach takes you aside to talk.

"You're a great fielder," he says, "no question about that. I've never seen a kid get on top of the ball the way you do. But you need to practice your hitting more."

"I will, Coach," you say. "I'll give it everything I got. Someday I'd like to break into the majors."

The coach drapes his big hand over your shoulder. "Maybe you'll make the starting lineup here at school, but the big leagues isn't in the cards for you, kid—I'm sorry. You just don't have the talent."

You nod. You hate to hear those words, but you're glad he didn't beat around the bush.

The coach looks off into space. "Yeah," he muses, "in a way it's too bad you didn't stick to skateboarding. I saw you skating around the fountain a couple of times—you were fantastic."

"Thanks, Coach."

"It's a shame—I think you could have been a skateboard champion."

The End

ABOUT THE AUTHOR

EDWARD PACKARD is a graduate of Princeton University and Columbia Law School. He developed the unique storytelling approach used in the Choose Your Own Adventure series while thinking up stories for his children, Caroline, Andrea, and Wells.

ABOUT THE ILLUSTRATOR

RON WING is a cartoonist and illustrator who has contributed to many publications. For the past several years he has illustrated the Bantam humor series of Larry Wilde's "Official" joke books. In addition, he has illustrated many books in Bantam's Choose Your Own Adventure series, including *You Are a Millionaire,* as well as titles in the Skylark Choose Your Own Adventure series, including *Haunted Halloween Party, A Day with the Dinosaurs, Spooky Thanksgiving,* and *You Are Invisible.* Mr. Wing now lives and works in Benton, Pennsylvania.

CHOOSE YOUR OWN ADVENTURE®

Choosy Kids Choose

CHOOSE YOUR OWN ADVENTURE ®
